First Edition
10 9 8 7 6 5 4 3 2 1
ISBN 978-1-4231-8656-4
F322-8368-0-14017
Printed in the USA
For more Disney Press fun, visit www.disneybooks.com

Sofia
the First

The
Enchanted
Feast

Adapted by

Catherine Hapka

Based on the episode written by

Craig Gerber and Michael G. Stern

Illustrated by

Grace Lee

DISNEP PRESS

New York • Los Angeles

I'm Princess Sofia, and I am so excited!
Today we are playing croquet, waiting for the
Enchanted Feast to begin.

Baileywick interrupts our game to announce an unexpected visitor.

Baileywick presents Sascha the sorceress!
"I've come to pay my respects to the great
King Roland," the sorceress says.

She conjures up a **new** scepter for Dad and some flowers for Mom . . .

pretty bracelets for Amber . . .

and **shiny** new boots for James!

Something about Sascha seems familiar.
"Have we met before?" I ask her.

"No," says Sascha, staring
strangely at my amulet.
"I'd remember such a
charming princess—
especially one with such a
beautiful amulet."

Then Sascha conjures up a necklace for me.

But I'd **never** take off my amulet,
so I give my new necklace to Amber.

Cedric arrives and introduces himself to Sascha.
"The Cedric the sorcerer?" she asks.
"It's an honor!"
Cedric blushes.

Mom and Dad invite Sascha to the **Enchanted Feast.** Everyone seems **SO** excited about Sascha, but something just doesn't seem right about her.

So I go to visit Cedric.

"I get a bad feeling around Sascha," I tell him.

"Since you're a sorcerer, too, I thought

you might know if she's up to something."

But Cedric just tells me to stop worrying. He thinks Sascha's great.

Then he shows me the trick he's planning for the feast.
With a flick of his wand, he fills the
entire room with mirrors.

But these aren't just any mirrors.
They're Morpho-Mirrors. "Wow! It looks like
I'm a totally different person in each one!" I exclaim.

Finally, the Enchanted Feast begins,
with guests from all over the kingdom.

Cedric makes a grand entrance
and gets ready for his trick.
He raises his wand. . . .

Poof!

The Morpho-Mirrors appear.
But then something goes wrong!
The mirrors **trap** Cedric,
bouncing him like a ball from
one mirror to the next!

Nobody knows what to do—except
Sascha. With one wave of her
wand, she makes the mirrors
disappear.

Then Sascha conjures up the most **amazing** food you've ever seen! Talk about an **enchanted** *feast!*

Everyone applauds for
Sascha the sorceress.
Well, everyone except Cedric,
who slinks quietly out of the room.
"Mr. Cedric, wait!" I call, running after him.

But Cedric disappears into his tower.
Poor Cedric. I feel so bad for him.
Clover hops up and asks me what's wrong.

"Everyone thinks the
new sorceress is great," I tell him.

"But **something** about her just doesn't seem right."

Then **my** **amulet** starts to glow!

And Snow White appears!
She sits down and begins to tell me a
story. "Once, an old woman gave me a
poisoned apple, but she was really my
wicked stepmother in disguise."

Snow White takes my hand.
"Sofia, people aren't always who they
pretend to be. If you get a bad feeling
about someone, you should trust
that feeling, no matter what."

Now I know what to do.

I've got to warn Mom and Dad about Sascha!

But when I reach the dining hall, Sascha is outside it and vines are blocking the doors!

Suddenly . . .

she transforms.

Now I know why she seemed so familiar.

"Miss Nettle!" I cry.

Miss Nettle is a very bad fairy. Once, she tried to steal a spell book from the good fairies, but I stopped her. "What are you doing here?" I ask.

"I've come for the
Amulet of Avalor!"
Miss Nettle cackles.

She tries to grab
my amulet, but I
run away from her.

I make it to the Great Hall and find
Cedric there, practicing his Morpho-Mirror trick.
Luckily, this time it's working perfectly!

Miss Nettle finds us there.

"You want the amulet?" I say.

"Come and get it!"

Miss Nettle flings a spell at me. . . . At least, she **thinks** it's me. But it's really a mirror—so the spell bounces back and traps the bad fairy with her own magic!

But Miss Nettle escapes the trap.

"You haven't seen the last of me!" she cries as she flies through the window.

Whew!

Now that she's gone, we
can all just have fun with
Cedric's **amazing**
Morpho-Mirrors!

I really hope Miss Nettle
never comes back. But if she does,
I'll be ready—thanks to the advice from my
new friend
Snow White.

The
End

Use these reusable stickers to decorate the poster of

Sofia and Clover in the garden.